SALLY

Written by Greg Stelzer

Illustrated by Mel Barren

Archway Publishing books may be ordered through booksellers or by contacting:

Archway Publishing
1663 Liberty Drive
Bloomington, IN 47403
www.archwaypublishing.com
1 (888) 242-5904

Because of the dynamic nature of the Internet, any web addresses or links contained in
this book may have changed since publication and may no longer be valid. The views
expressed in this work are solely those of the author and do not necessarily reflect the
views of the publisher, and the publisher hereby disclaims any responsibility for them.

Any people depicted in stock imagery provided by Getty Images are models,
and such images are being used for illustrative purposes only.
Certain stock imagery © Getty Images.

ISBN: 978-1-4808-8807-4 (sc)
ISBN: 9781480888081 (hc)
ISBN: 978-1-4808-8806-7 (e)

Print information available on the last page.

Archway Publishing rev. date: 04/16/2020

Sally learns she is afraid of heights and must find a way to overcome her fear.

Determined to overcome her fear, Sally spends most of her days down in the woods flying low to the ground until an accident changes everything!

This book will have you turning the pages to find out what happens to Sally in the woods.

This book is dedicated to Sara

This is the story of Sally.
Sally is a bird. Not just any bird. She is a hawk!

Hawks spend their days in tall trees
and fly high in the sky.

When it was time for Sally's first flying lesson, she was hopping around in excitement.

Her parents guided her to the edge of the nest and Sally hopped onto the edge.

As soon
as Sally
looked
down,
her heart
started to
race and
she felt
dizzy.

Her eyes opened wide and she shrieked.

"WHOAAAAAA!"
Sally fell backwards and
fainted!

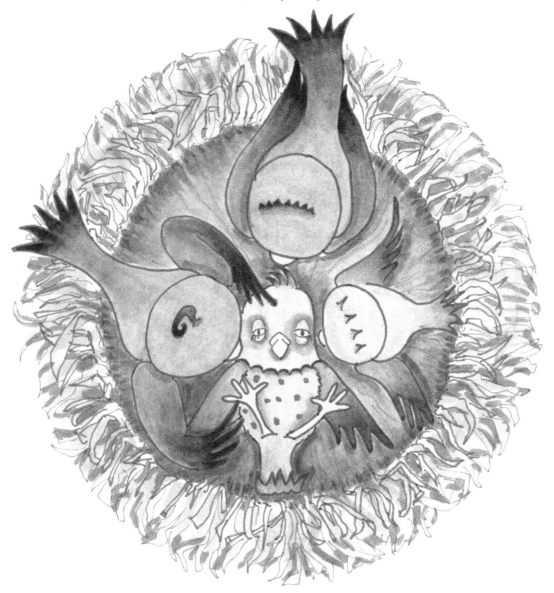

When she woke up, her mom was leaning down,
fanning her. "What happened?" asked Sally.
"You fainted" said her mom.

Sally hopped to the edge of the nest again, determined to fly like her mom and dad. "WHOAAAAAA!" cried Sally and fainted again!

When she woke up her little brother, Roger was pointing and laughing at her.

"Stop laughing at me!" cried Sally as tears started to form.
"Stop teasing your sister Roger" said Sally's mom as she
helped her up and put her wing around her.

"What's wrong with me?" cried Sally.
Her dad paced around in thought. Then he
stopped and looked at Sally. "I know why you
fainted . . . you are afraid of heights!"

This is a big problem! Actually, for Sally it's a HUGE problem because hawks spend most of their time high in trees or towers. And they soar in the sky hundreds of feet above the ground.

Sally looked at her dad. "But I'm a hawk and we are not supposed to be afraid of heights!"
"That's true sweetheart" replied her dad. Roger jumped in front of Sally and yelled, "Sally is a scaredy-cat!"

"Stop that!" ordered his father. Then to Sally he said, "Sally, I will help you overcome your fear of heights."

The very next day, Sally hopped on her dad's back and closed her eyes while he glided them down to the ground.

"Try and fly a few feet off the ground to get used to your wings" said her dad.

So, she flapped her wings and flew a few feet before losing control and tumbling to the ground.

Sally got up and said, "That was fun!" She flew a little higher and farther before she got scared and came back down with a hard landing.

Sally did this for several days until she got the hang of flying. But she wouldn't fly higher than the trees for fear of fainting again.

As the days turned into weeks, Sally got really good at flying.

Roger, now older, learned to fly and was flying high in the sky with his father. He never flew in the woods with Sally because he said that was for chickens.

One day, Roger came down to watch Sally practice.

Roger was amazed! He had never seen a hawk dart around trees with such ability. He was very impressed but would not let her know.

Sally saw Roger and flew back to him, making a perfect landing right next to him. "Hi brother! Want to race me?"

"Sure! Are we going to race in the sky?" said Roger. Sally replied, "No silly, you know I am afraid of heights. Let's race to the edge of the woods."

Roger thought for a moment. "That's a long way and there are lots of trees!" Roger had never flown that low to the ground before, much less through trees. He was nervous.

Sally looked at her brother and said,
"Who's the scaredy-cat now?"
"I'm not scared . . . let's do it!" said Roger

At the count of three they took off.
Sally sped away with no fear. Roger tried
to keep up but he was afraid of crashing.

On they flew, Sally expertly through the woods. Roger was losing ground on Sally so he sped up, ignoring his fear.

Sally burst out of the woods!
. . . She won! . . . She was so excited!

Sally was so busy celebrating she didn't realize that Roger had not come out of the woods.

She flew back into the woods calling out to her brother. "Roger! Roger! Where are you?"

She flew faster, desperate to find her baby brother! Passing a big tree, she saw him on the ground with a damaged wing.

"Roger! What happened?!" shouted Sally. Roger looked up as she landed by his side. "I went faster to catch you but lost control and crashed into a tree. I think my wing is broken!" He tried to hold back the tears, but the pain was awful.

Sally was worried for her brother.
She needed to find their dad.
"Roger, try not to move,
I'm going to get Dad!"

Without a second thought, Sally
shot straight up into the air!
She flew as fast as she could
. . . up . . . up, past the
trees into the
clear blue
sky.

She spotted her dad high in the sky soaring in the wind. When Sally got closer, she cried out, "Dad! Dad!" Her dad turned, surprised to see Sally flying so high. He was going to congratulate her but realized something was not right.

"What's wrong?" he asked.
Sally slowed down and told him what had happened to Roger. Her dad listened then said, "Take me to Roger." Sally turned and dove, her father close behind.

As they darted around trees, Sally's dad was amazed and nervous because Sally was flying so fast and he had little experience in the woods.

He was worried she would hit a tree but then realized he was more likely to hit a tree than Sally. So, he slowed down.

Once he got to Roger, Sally was already by his side telling him everything was going to be alright.

"It's my fault Roger got hurt!" cried Sally.
"I challenged him to a race in the woods."

Sally looked at Roger. "I'm so sorry baby brother!" as she started to cry. "It's ok Sally, I'm sorry I called you a scaredy-cat," said Roger.

Father was pleased they apologized to each other and said, "Let's get you back home so mom can fix your wing."

Sally helped Roger onto their father's back and slowly flew out of the forest and to their nest. Half way up, Roger looked down to the ground then at Sally who was flying next to them. "Hey Sally! Look how high you are!" yelled Roger.

Sally looked down.
"Wha . . . ?!"

. . . She didn't faint! . . . She felt fine! After a moment she cried out,

"Wow! Look at me! I'm flying like a hawk!"

Sally started to laugh joyfully as she flew in circles around her dad and brother. They were proud of her.

Once Roger was bandaged up, Sally's mom turned to her and said, "I'm very proud of you Sally. You were so concerned about your brother, you forgot about your fear of heights."

Her dad spoke up and said, "Sally, all you needed was confidence. Flying in the woods gave you the practice and strength you needed to fly. When Roger got hurt, you reacted confidently and skilfully without thinking. That was a brave thing to do".

Roger looked at his parents with pride and said, "You should have seen Sally flying in the woods! She was so

fast and

fearless!"

From that day forward, Sally wasn't afraid of heights. She realized that with lots of practice and confidence she could do anything!

Like the proud hawk she was, she spent her days flying with her brother and parents high in the sky.

When she missed flying in the woods, Sally would dive down and fly around the trees with a skill never before seen by other hawks. Sally even taught her brother to do the same . . . but in a safe manner, of course!

The End

Printed in the USA
CPSIA information can be obtained
at www.ICGtesting.com
LVHW071728011123
762562LV00014B/724